Rotraut Susanne Berner
DEFINITELY
NOT
for
Little Ones

First published as *Rotraut Susanne Berners Märchencomics*

English-language edition published in Canada and the USA in 2009 by Groundwood Books

Groundwood Books / House of Anansi Press
110 Spadina Avenue, Suite 801, Toronto, Ontario M5V 2K4
or c/o Publishers Group West
1700 Fourth Street, Berkeley, CA 94710

We acknowledge for their financial support of our publishing program the Government of Canada through the Book Publishing Industry Development Program (BPIDP).

Library and Archives Canada Cataloguing in Publication
Berner, Rotraut Susanne
Definitely not for little ones : some very Grimm fairy-tale comics / Rotraut Susanne Berner ;
Translation of: Märchencomics.
ISBN 978-0-88899-957-3
1. Fairy tales–Germany. 2. Fairy tales. 3. Folklore–Germany.
I. Grimm, Jacob, 1785-1863 II. Grimm, Wilhelm, 1786-1859
III. Title.
PZ8.B44De 2008 j398.20943 C2009-901069-0

The illustrations are in color pencil and watercolor.
Printed and bound in China

THE
FROG PRINCE
ONCE UPON A TIME THERE WAS A KING...
WHO HAD FOUR BEAUTIFUL DAUGHTERS, BUT THE YOUNGEST WAS THE MOST BEAUTIFUL OF THEM ALL.
ON WARM DAYS SHE LOVED TO GO TO THE COOL FOUNTAIN, WHERE SHE WOULD PLAY WITH HER GOLDEN BALL.

THEN ONE DAY...
OH, NO!
KERPLUNK!
SOB!
RIBBIT! WHAT WILL YOU GIVE ME IF I FETCH YOUR BALL?
ANYTHING! PEARLS, PRECIOUS JEWELS, MY GOLDEN CROWN...
RIBBIT! I DON'T WANT ANY OF THAT STUFF! I WANT TO SIT AT YOUR TABLE, EAT FROM YOUR PLATE, DRINK FROM YOUR CUP AND SLEEP IN YOUR BED!
I PROMISE!

RIBBIT! RIBBIT!
HEY, TAKE ME WITH YOU!!
SLAM!
BANG!
WHO'S THAT CALLING YOU?
KNOCK, KNOCK!
OH, YOUNGEST PRINCESS! LET ME IN!

IT'S THIS HIDEOUS FROG WHO FETCHED MY GOLDEN BALL OUT OF THE FOUNTAIN. I PROMISED HIM THAT HE COULD BE MY FRIEND, BUT I DIDN'T THINK HE'D TAKE IT SERIOUSLY.
IF YOU MADE A PROMISE, YOU MUST KEEP IT!
RIBBIT! LET ME IN!
RIBBIT, RIBBIT!
PICK ME UP! RIBBIT!
LET ME EAT FROM YOUR PLATE! RIBBIT!
I'M TIRED. TAKE ME TO YOUR ROOM! RIBBIT, RIBBIT!

A SHORT TIME LATER...
PUT ME IN YOUR BED!
THAT'S THE LAST STRAW!
BANG!
SPLAT!
WHO ARE YOU?
I AM A PRINCE. A WICKED WITCH TURNED ME INTO A FROG, AND YOU HAVE RELEASED ME FROM HER SPELL. WILL YOU MARRY ME?
AND THEY WOULD STILL BE ALIVE TODAY...
IF THEY HADN'T DIED, THAT IS.

MOTHER HOLLE

ONCE UPON A TIME THERE WAS A WIDOW WHO HAD TWO DAUGHTERS.
ONE WAS HER STEPDAUGHTER. ALL DAY LONG SHE HAD TO WASH, CLEAN AND SPIN, WHILE THE OTHER DAUGHTER WAS ALLOWED TO LAZE AROUND.
ONE DAY...
OH, NO! I'VE PRICKED MY FINGER AND NOW THE SPOOL IS ALL BLOODY! I'D BETTER WASH IT OFF IN THE WELL!
OOPS!
UH-OH!
COCK-A-DOODLE-DOO!
SOB!
YOU WILL GO AND FETCH THAT SPOOL OUT OF THE WELL!

HELP!
HELP!
HELP!
HELP!
NOT MUCH LATER...
WHERE AM I?
PULL ME OUT, PULL ME OUT, BEFORE I BURN!
MANY THANKS!
SHAKE ME!
WE'RE ALL RIPE!
THANK YOU!
THANKS!
THANKS!
THANKS!
THANKS!
THANKS!
THANK YOU!

NOT LONG AFTER...
WHAT ARE YOU AFRAID OF, DEAR CHILD? I AM MOTHER HOLLE. YOU CAN STAY WITH ME IF YOU WORK HARD. HELP ME SHAKE OUT THE BEDDING. THEN IT WILL SNOW IN THE WORLD!
WEEKS LATER...
EVEN THOUGH I AM SO HAPPY HERE, I WOULD REALLY LIKE TO GO HOME.
YOU'VE SERVED ME LOYALLY. COME WITH ME.
GOLD
THIS IS THE REWARD FOR YOUR FAITHFUL SERVICE.
COCK-A-DOODLE-DOO! OUR GOLDEN GIRL HAS COME BACK!
YOU WILL DO EVERYTHING EXACTLY THE WAY YOUR SISTER DID AND COME BACK JUST AS RICH AND BEAUTIFUL.
YES, MOTHER.

OUCH!
?
INTO THE WELL YOU GO!
WHERE AM I?
PULL ME OUT, PULL ME OUT, OR ELSE I WILL BURN!
I'M NOT GOING TO GET SOOT ALL OVER ME!
SHAKE ME!
WE ARE ALL RIPE!
PHOOEY! IF I DO, ONE MIGHT FALL ON MY HEAD!
I WANT TO WORK FOR YOU.
GOOD, YOU CAN START RIGHT AWAY.

DAY 1
DAY 2
DAY 3
DAY 4
THIS IS NO GOOD. IT'S NOON ALREADY!
I'M GOING TO TAKE YOU BACK HOME.
OH, YES, PLEASE!
TAR
THIS IS YOUR REWARD FOR YOUR SERVICE!
COCK-A-DOODLE-DOO! OUR DIRTY GIRL HAS COME BACK!
SCRUB, SCRUB.
BUT SHE COULD NOT SCRUB OFF THE TAR, AND IT STAYED ON HER FOR EVER AFTER.

Tom Thumb

ONCE UPON A TIME THERE WAS A FARMER AND HIS WIFE...
IT IS SO SAD THAT WE HAVE NO CHILDREN. OUR HOUSE IS SO QUIET, BUT OTHER HOMES ARE NOISY AND HAPPY.
I KNOW. IF ONLY WE HAD JUST ONE CHILD, EVEN ONE THAT WAS NO BIGGER THAN A THUMB!
SEVEN MONTHS LATER...
WE WILL CALL YOU TOM THUMB, AND YOU WILL BE OUR DARLING CHILD.
ONE YEAR LATER...
FIVE YEARS LATER...
SEVEN YEAR LATER...
I'M GOING TO THE FOREST. OH, WOULDN'T IT BE NICE IF SOMEONE COULD BRING THE HORSE AND WAGON!
ONE MORNING...
AND JUST HOW IS THAT GOING TO WORK?
FATHER, I CAN DO THAT!
I'LL SIT INSIDE THE HORSE'S EAR!

IN THE AFTERNOON...
BE CAREFUL, TOM THUMB!
LET'S JUST HOPE THIS WORKS!
THANKS, MOTHER!
AT THE EDGE OF THE FOREST
WHAT THE...?? NO ONE'S DRIVING THAT WAGON!
SOMETHING'S NOT RIGHT HERE. LET'S GO AND SEE!
GIDDYUP!
IN THE FOREST...
YOU SEE, FATHER, HOW WELL THAT WENT? NOW PLEASE HELP ME DOWN.
TOM THUMB! I AM PROUD OF YOU.
NO ONE'S GOING TO BELIEVE THIS!
WE COULD MAKE A FORTUNE OFF THAT GUY!
HELLO! WE'D LIKE TO BUY THAT LITTLE MAN FROM YOU.
NEVER!
NOT FOR ALL THE GOLD IN THE WORLD.
PSST, FATHER. GO AHEAD AND SELL ME. I CAN FIND MY WAY HOME AGAIN!

OKAY. I'LL DO IT.
HERE'S THE MONEY FOR YOUR LITTLE DARLING.
SHORTLY AFTER...
I HAVE TO GO PEE!
AS FAR AS I'M CONCERNED YOU CAN TAKE CARE OF IT UP THERE!
NO! AFTER ALL, I KNOW THE PROPER WAY TO DO THINGS.
LET ME DOWN!
SO LONG, GENTLEMEN. YOU'RE NOT GOING TO SEE ME AGAIN!
HEE-HEE! STRAIGHT FOR THE MOUSE HOLE!
RATS, HE TRICKED US. WE'LL NEVER FIND HIM AGAIN.
ONE HOUR LATER...
THE AIR IS CLEAN, BUT IT'S TOO DANGEROUS HERE...
...OH, A SNAIL HOUSE! I'LL BE SAFE IN THERE!
LATER...
I'VE BEEN THINKING ABOUT HOW WE CAN TAKE MONEY FROM THE RICH VICAR IN THE VILLAGE...
I CAN SHOW YOU HOW!
WHO SAID THAT?
I'M RIGHT HERE! I CAN HELP YOU BECAUSE I'M SO SMALL, I CAN SNEAK THROUGH ANY WINDOW!

OKAY, LET'S SEE WHAT YOU CAN DO...
A SHORT TIME LATER...
DO YOU WANT EVERYTHING THAT'S IN HERE?
HAS HE GONE CRAZY? HE'S GOING TO WAKE UP THE ENTIRE VILLAGE! LET'S GET OUT OF HERE!
IN THE MAID'S ROOM...
WHAT'S THAT RACKET?
NOBODY'S THERE.
THAT'S WEIRD.
HEE-HEE. FIRST I'LL HAVE A GOOD SLEEP AND THEN I'LL GO BACK HOME.
A LOVELY PLACE TO SLEEP!
SUDDENLY...
IT'S GETTING CRAMPED IN HERE! STOP! NO MORE HAY!
WHOA! WHERE AM I?
...NO MORE HAY!
HELP! THAT'S THE SAME VOICE I HEARD LAST NIGHT! VICAR, HELP ME! THE COW IS TALKING!

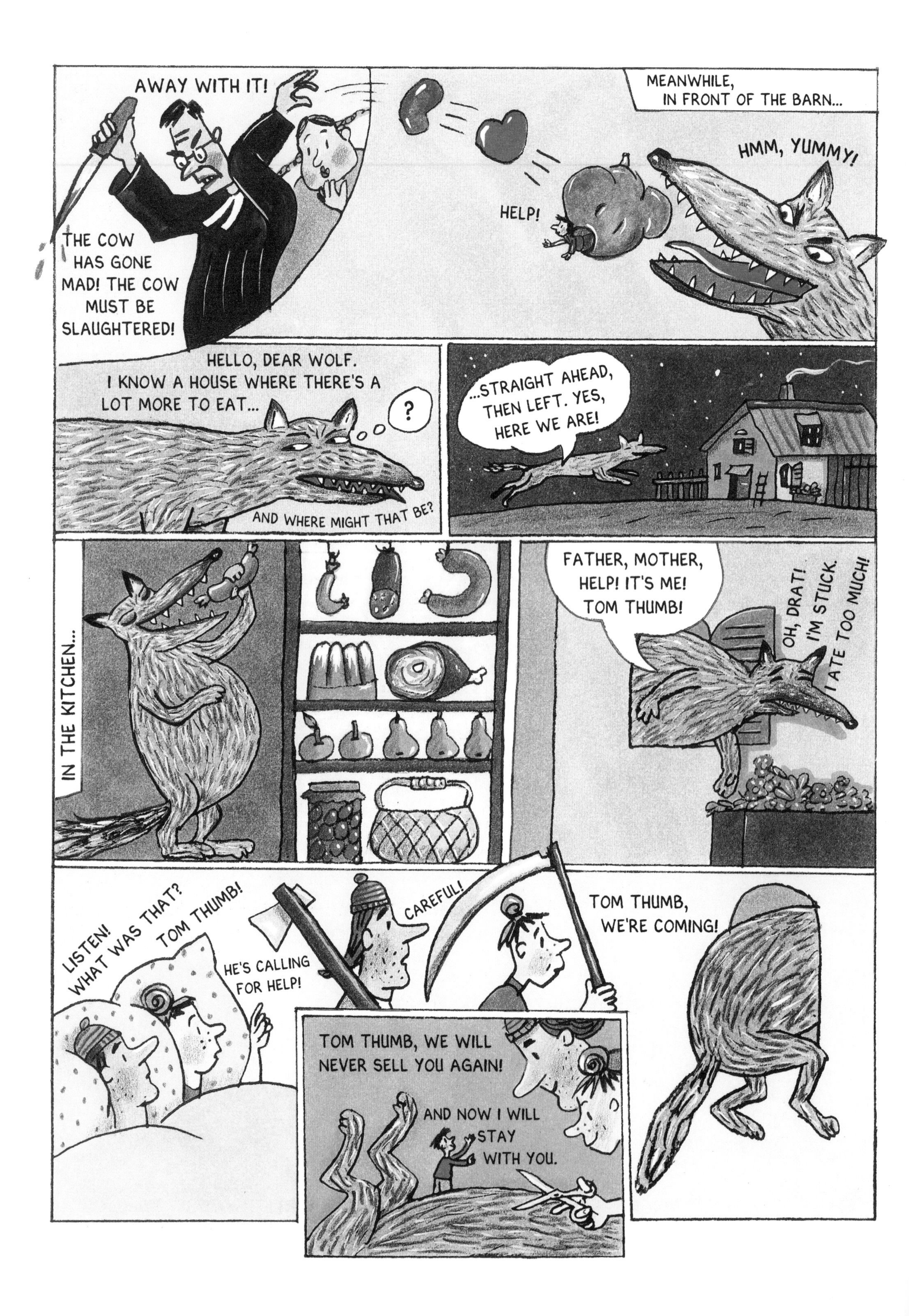
AWAY WITH IT!
THE COW HAS GONE MAD! THE COW MUST BE SLAUGHTERED!
MEANWHILE, IN FRONT OF THE BARN...
HMM, YUMMY!
HELP!
HELLO, DEAR WOLF. I KNOW A HOUSE WHERE THERE'S A LOT MORE TO EAT...
?
AND WHERE MIGHT THAT BE?
...STRAIGHT AHEAD, THEN LEFT. YES, HERE WE ARE!
IN THE KITCHEN...
FATHER, MOTHER, HELP! IT'S ME! TOM THUMB!
OH, DRAT! I'M STUCK. I ATE TOO MUCH!
LISTEN! WHAT WAS THAT?
TOM THUMB!
HE'S CALLING FOR HELP!
CAREFUL!
TOM THUMB, WE'RE COMING!
TOM THUMB, WE WILL NEVER SELL YOU AGAIN!
AND NOW I WILL STAY WITH YOU.

RAPUNZEL
ONCE UPON A TIME THERE WAS A HUSBAND AND WIFE...
WHO WERE HAPPILY EXPECTING THEIR FIRST CHILD.
ONE DAY...
OH, LOOK AT THAT WONDERFUL LETTUCE!
I ABSOLUTELY MUST HAVE SOME!
SWEETHEART, WHAT'S THE MATTER?
LETTUCE!
LATER...

THE NEXT DAY...
SWEETHEART, WHAT'S THE MATTER?
LETTUCE!
TOWARD EVENING...
SUDDENLY...
HOW DARE YOU STEAL MY LETTUCE!
MERCY!
AS PUNISHMENT YOU WILL GIVE ME YOUR CHILD!
YES, OKAY.
A FEW WEEKS LATER...
MY RAPUNZEL!
AND SO...

YEARS LATER...
RAPUNZEL HAS BECOME THE MOST BEAUTIFUL CHILD UNDER THE SUN.
ONE DAY...
FROM NOW ON YOU WILL LIVE IN THIS TOWER WITH NO DOOR AND NO STAIRS!
SIGH!
EVERY MORNING...
RAPUNZEL, RAPUNZEL, LET DOWN YOUR HAIR!
OH, BROTHER, NOT AGAIN!
AND AT NOON...
GOODBYE, RAPUNZEL! UNTIL TOMORROW!
ONE MORNING...
DO YOU HEAR THAT BEAUTIFUL VOICE, ROSA?
THAT'S FUNNY, I CAN'T FIND THE DOOR.

SHHH, I HEAR FOOTSTEPS!
RAPUNZEL, RAPUNZEL, LET DOWN YOUR HAIR!
LATER THAT NIGHT...
RAPUNZEL, RAPUNZEL, LET DOWN YOUR HAIR!
WHO ARE YOU?
UNTIL TOMORROW NIGHT, RAPUNZEL. GOOD NIGHT!
THE NEXT MORNING...
YOU SURE ARE A LOT HEAVIER THAN MY PRINCE!
?
WHAT PRINCE?!!
OOPS!
AWAY WITH YOU. NOW YOU'RE ON YOUR OWN!
SNIP!
HEH, HEH, HEH. WON'T THE PRINCE BE SURPRISED!

A SHORT TIME LATER...
WHAT ARE YOU STARING AT?
YOU WILL NEVER SEE RAPUNZEL AGAIN!
ACK!
HEH, HEH, HEH.
HELP! THE THORNS...
THE THORNS HAVE PIERCED MY EYES. I AM BLIND!
OH, RAPUNZEL, HOW WILL I EVER FIND YOU AGAIN?
YEARS LATER...
LISTEN, ROSA! ISN'T THAT RAPUNZEL'S VOICE?
SOB!
MY DARLING RAPUNZEL! I HAVE FOUND YOU AT LAST!
?
?
YOUR TEARS HAVE HEALED ME! I CAN SEE AGAIN!
AND NOW YOU CAN SEE OUR TWINS.
DADDY!
DAD!
AND THEY WOULD STILL BE ALIVE TODAY
... IF THEY HADN'T DIED, THAT IS.

JORINDA & JORINDEL

ONCE UPON A TIME THERE WAS AN OLD CASTLE DEEP IN THE FOREST, AND IN IT LIVED A WITCH. SHE COULD TRANSFORM HERSELF INTO AN OWL OR A CAT BY DAY, AND SHE COULD TURN INNOCENT MAIDENS INTO BIRDS...

DEAREST JORINDA, STAY AWAY FROM THE WITCH AND DON'T GO TOO NEAR THE CASTLE. SHE'S ALREADY TURNED 7,000 MAIDENS INTO BIRDS!

YES, JORINDEL, BUT YOU MUST ALSO TAKE CARE, BECAUSE IF YOU GO WITHIN 100 STEPS OF THE CASTLE, THE WITCH WILL PUT A SPELL ON YOU AND YOU WILL NOT BE ABLE TO MOVE.

THEN ONE AFTERNOON...
OH, NO! WE GOT LOST! IT'S THE CASTLE!
THEN, SUDDENLY...
HOO-HOO! HOO-HOO!
TWEET...
JORINDA? WHERE ARE YOU?

HEE, HEE, HEE! NOW I'VE GOT YOU, JORINDA!
I CAN'T MOVE!
LATER THAT NIGHT...
I WILL FREE YOU.
O, ZACHIEL WHEN THE MOON SHINES ON THE CAGE
LET HIM LOOSE AT ONCE!
OH, PLEASE, I BEG YOU! GIVE ME BACK MY JORINDA!
YOU WILL NEVER SEE HER AGAIN!

SOB!
WHAT AM I GOING TO DO? HOW WILL I FIND JORINDA?
LATER THAT NIGHT, IN A DREAM...
1
2
3
4
AND SO THE NEXT MORNING...
I MUST FIND THAT RED FLOWER!
DAY 1
DAY 2
DAY 3
DAY 4
DAY 5
THE RED FLOWER! I'VE FOUND IT!
DAY 6
DAY 7
DAY 8
DAY 9

IT'S JUST LIKE MY DREAM. THE SPELL IS BROKEN. I AM FREE TO GO INTO THE CASTLE!
IT WORKS! THE FLOWER OPENS THE DOOR!
TWEET!
PEEP!
PEEP!
WARBLE!
CHIRP!
STOP!
GRRR!
CHIRP!
YOU HAVE NO MORE POWER!
TWEET!
WARBLE!
HURRAY!
HURRAY FOR JORINDEL!
I WAS A NIGHTINGALE!
I WAS A BLACKBIRD!
HE FREED US ALL!
YAY!
PEEP!
AND THEY LIVED TOGETHER HAPPILY FOR A LONG TIME.
MEEOW

LUCKY HANS
MY DEAR HANS. YOU HAVE SERVED ME FAITHFULLY FOR SEVEN YEARS. TAKE THIS GOLD AS YOUR REWARD.
THANKS.
ON THE WAY HOME...
YIKES, THIS GOLD IS HEAVY!
WHY ARE YOU ON FOOT, HANS? I'LL GIVE YOU MY WHOLE HORSE FOR YOUR TINY BIT OF GOLD!
IT MUST BE NICE TO BE CARRIED BY A HORSE LIKE THAT.

HA HA HA...
GIDDYUP!
NEIGH!
OW!
OH!
MOOOO!
RIBBIT!
I'M NEVER GETTING ON A HORSE AGAIN! WHAT I WOULDN'T GIVE FOR A COW! THEN I WOULD HAVE MILK, BUTTER AND CHEESE EVERY DAY.
AS A FAVOR, I'LL TRADE YOU MY COW FOR YOUR HORSE.
HEE, HEE, HEE...

OW! I WANTED TO MILK THE COW, BUT SHE WON'T GIVE ME ANY!
YOU'VE BEEN CHEATED! THAT COW IS MUCH TOO OLD. BUT SINCE I FEEL SORRY FOR YOU, I'LL TRADE YOU MY YOUNG PIG FOR YOUR OLD COW.
HEH, HEH, HEH!
OINK!

HELLO, YOU! THE POLICE IN TOWN ARE LOOKING FOR A PIG THIEF. I'LL HELP YOU. I'LL TRADE YOU THAT PIG FOR MY GOOSE. THAT WAY YOU WON'T BE ARRESTED.
OH, THANK YOU SO MUCH!
HO, HO, HO!
ROAST GOOSE, GOOSE FAT, SOFT FEATHERS FOR MY BED...
I SHARPEN THE SHEARS AND TURN LIKE THE WIND...

THIS BUSINESS IS A GOLD MINE. A KNIFE SHARPENER LIKE ME ALWAYS HAS MONEY IN HIS POCKET, HANS. AND ALL YOU NEED IS A GRINDSTONE. HERE, TAKE THESE.
OH, THANK YOU! I'LL TRADE THE GOOSE FOR YOUR STONES!
ACK!
GROAN!
I'M THIRSTY!
OH!
OOPS!
SPLASH!
OH, WHAT LUCK! I FEEL SO MUCH LIGHTER NOW!
MY HANS!
MOTHER!

Hans the Hedgehog
ONCE UPON A TIME THERE WAS A FARMER...
THE PEOPLE IN TOWN ARE LAUGHING AT ME. I WANT TO HAVE A CHILD, EVEN IF IT TURNS OUT TO BE A HEDGEHOG.
NINE MONTHS LATER...
WAAAH!
WE'LL CALL HIM HANS THE HEDGEHOG.
FOR EIGHT YEARS HANS THE HEDGEHOG LIVED BEHIND THE STOVE.
SIGH...
ONE DAY...
I'M GOING INTO TOWN. WHAT SHALL I BRING YOU?
MEAT AND BREAD, PLEASE!
BRING ME BAGPIPES!
SO THAT EVENING...
PLEASE GIVE ME A COUPLE OF DONKEYS AND PIGS AND I WILL RIDE AWAY AND NEVER RETURN.
I'M GLAD WE'RE FINALLY RID OF HIM!

ONE NIGHT, YEARS LATER...
WE'VE LOST OUR WAY! BUT WHERE IS THAT MUSIC COMING FROM?
I'LL SHOW YOU THE WAY HOME IF YOU PROMISE TO GIVE ME THE FIRST THING YOU MEET WHEN YOU GET THERE, BUT I MUST HAVE IT IN WRITING.
OKAY.
HEEHAW
OINK
OINK
I'M NOT PROMISING HIM ANYTHING. HE CAN'T EVEN READ!
DAD!

THE KING TOLD HIS DAUGHTER ABOUT HANS THE HEDGEHOG AND THE FAKE AGREEMENT.
ONE NIGHT, MONTHS LATER...
WE'VE LOST OUR WAY. BUT WHERE IS THAT MUSIC COMING FROM?
I'LL SHOW YOU THE WAY HOME IF YOU PROMISE TO GIVE ME THE FIRST THING YOU MEET WHEN YOU GET THERE, BUT I MUST HAVE IT IN WRITING.

FATHER!
AND HE TOLD HER ABOUT HANS THE HEDGEHOG AND THE CONTRACT.
I'M SO SORRY!
FOR YOUR SAKE I'LL GO WITH HIM.
ONE MORNING, MONTHS LATER...
I'VE HAD ENOUGH OF LOOKING AFTER ANIMALS. LET'S GO BACK TO THE CASTLE OF THE FIRST KING.
SNORT
NEIGH
GRUNT
OINK
COCK-A-DOODLE-DOO!
ISN'T THAT HANS THE HEDGEHOG? THE ONE WE'RE SUPPOSED TO SHOOT DOWN, CUT DOWN AND STAB? HE'S JUST FLYING OVER THE WALL!!!
KING, GIVE ME YOUR DAUGHTER OR I WILL TAKE BOTH YOUR LIVES!

SHORTLY AFTER...
THERE'S NO WAY AROUND IT. YOU HAVE TO GO.
GRRR...
THAT'S WHAT YOU GET FOR TRICKING ME! GET LOST! I DON'T WANT YOU!
INSIDE THE COACH...
HELP! HELP! HE'S PRICKED ME ALL OVER!
THEY RODE TO THE SECOND KINGDOM...

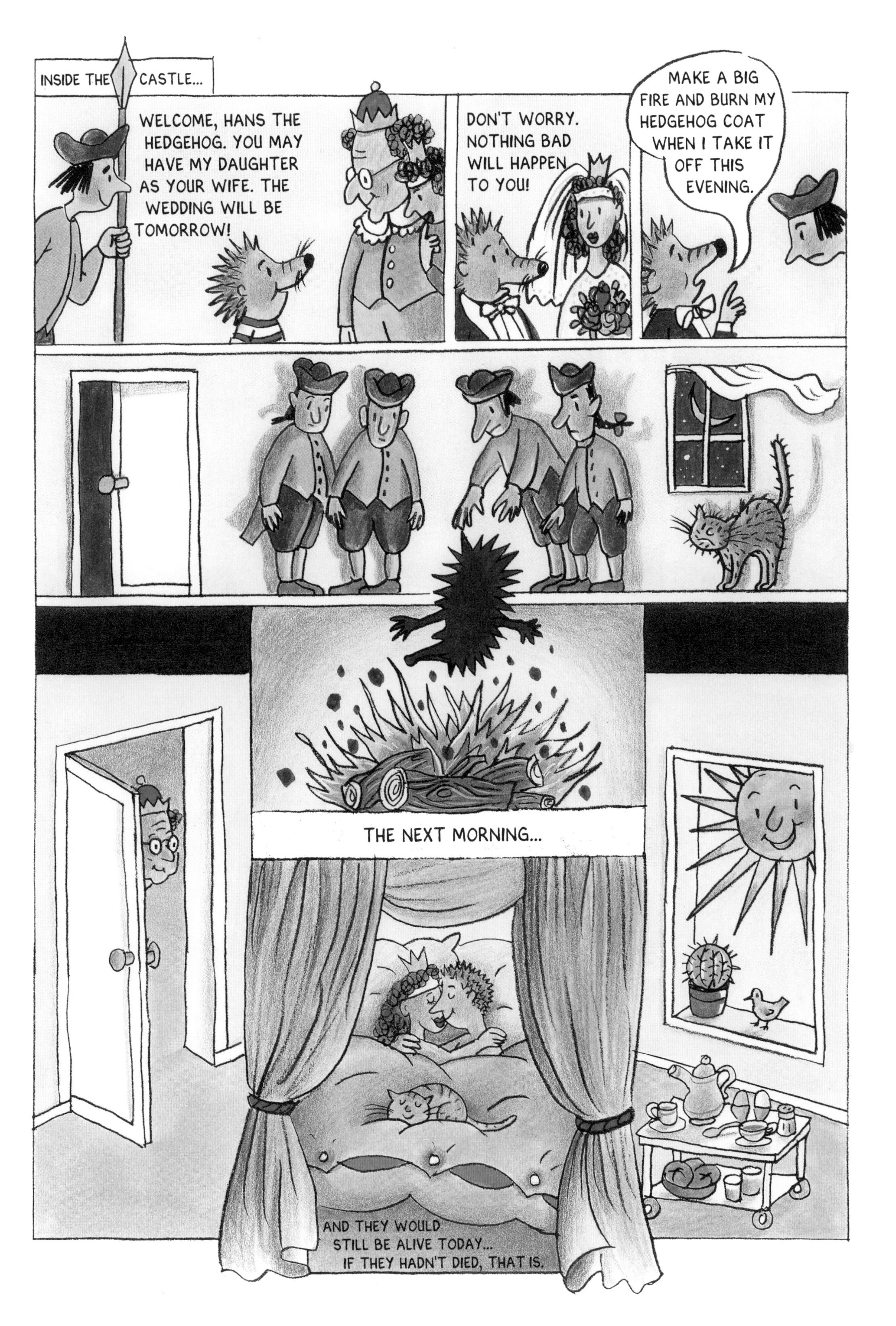
INSIDE THE CASTLE...
WELCOME, HANS THE HEDGEHOG. YOU MAY HAVE MY DAUGHTER AS YOUR WIFE. THE WEDDING WILL BE TOMORROW!
DON'T WORRY. NOTHING BAD WILL HAPPEN TO YOU!
MAKE A BIG FIRE AND BURN MY HEDGEHOG COAT WHEN I TAKE IT OFF THIS EVENING.
THE NEXT MORNING...
AND THEY WOULD STILL BE ALIVE TODAY... IF THEY HADN'T DIED, THAT IS.

LITTLE RED CAP
ONCE UPON A TIME...
LITTLE RED CAP!
THERE WAS A YOUNG
GIRL NAMED LITTLE RED CAP.
ONE DAY...
LITTLE RED CAP, PLEASE TAKE THIS WINE AND CAKE TO GRANDMOTHER'S HOUSE. SHE IS SICK. BUT PAY ATTENTION ON THE ROAD AND SPEAK TO NO ONE.
THE GRANDMOTHER LIVED A HALF HOUR AWAY, IN A SMALL CLEARING IN THE MIDDLE OF THE WOODS.

ON THE EDGE OF THE FOREST...
HELLO, THERE, LITTLE RED CAP. WHERE ARE YOU OFF TO?
TO MY GRANDMA'S.
AND WHERE DOES SHE LIVE?
OVER THERE IN THE CLEARING.
IN THE MEANTIME...
HELP!
HELP!
HELP!
HELP!
SHORTLY AFTER, IN GRANDMOTHER'S ROOM...
GRANDMA, WHAT BIG EARS YOU HAVE.
THE BETTER TO HEAR YOU WITH!
GRANDMA, WHAT BIG EYES YOU HAVE.
THE BETTER TO SEE YOU WITH!
GRANDMA, WHAT BIG HANDS YOU HAVE.
THE BETTER TO HOLD YOU WITH!
AND WHY DO YOU HAVE SUCH AN AWFULLY BIG MOUTH?
MEOW?

THE BETTER TO EAT
YOU WITH!
A SHORT TIME LATER...
SNORE...
SNORE... SNORE... SNORE...
TEN MINUTES LATER...
THERE WE GO!
SNORE...
OOF!

THEN...
PLOP!
PLOP!
PLOP!
SNORE...
SNORE...
LATER...
UGH...
GROAN...
GULP...
SPLAT!
HE'S DEAD!
THAT EVENING...
CHEERS!
CHEERS!
MEOW!
WOOF!
AND THEY WOULD STILL BE ALIVE TODAY... IF THEY HADN'T DIED, THAT IS.
THE END

Rotraut Susanne Berner
DEFINITELY
NOT
for
Little Ones